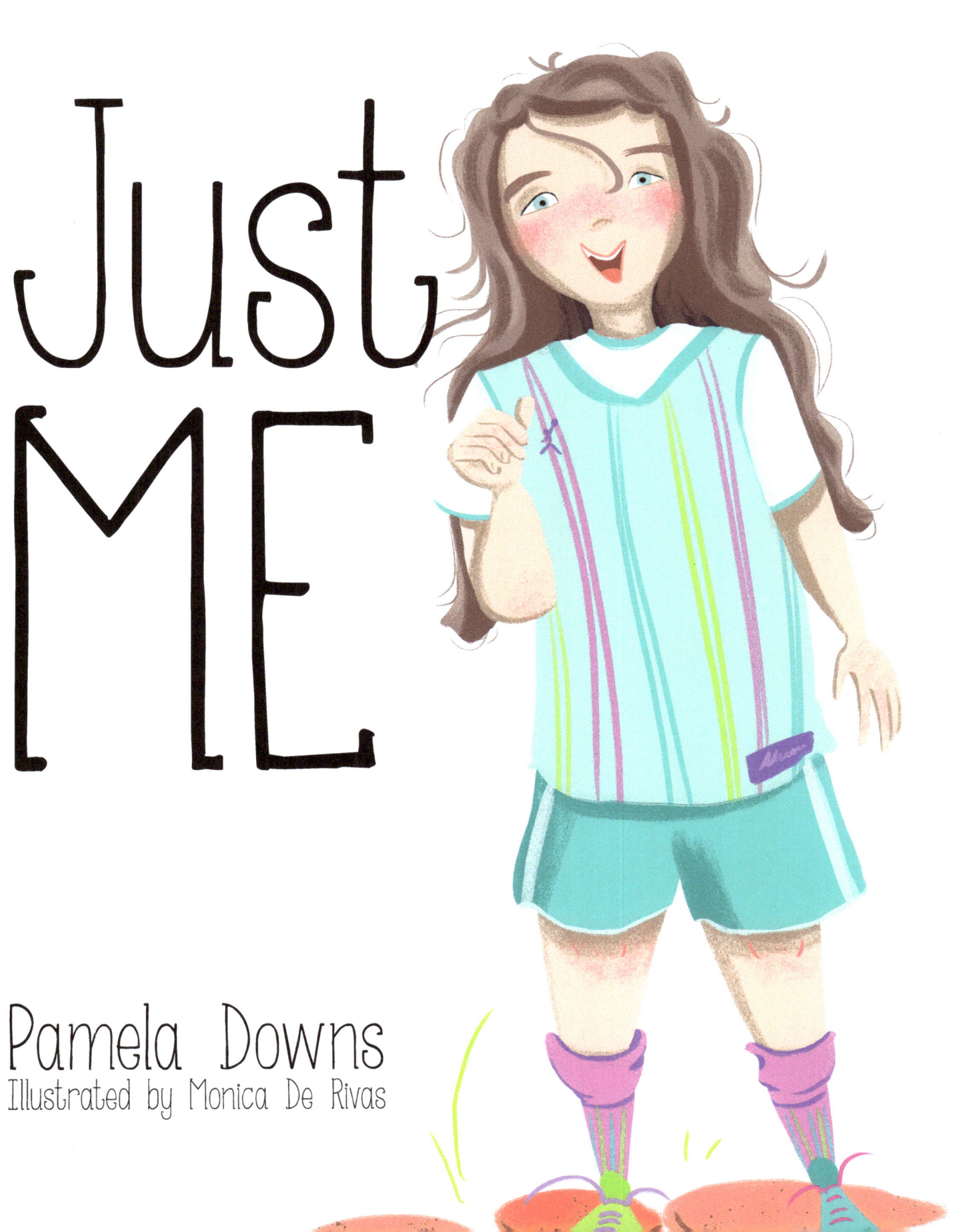

Copyright © 2024 by Pamela Downs. All rights reserved.
This book may not be reproduced or stored in whole or in part
by any means without the written permission of the author
except for brief quotations for the purpose of review.

ISBN: 978-1-963569-61-2 (hard cover)
978-1-963569-62-9 (soft cover)

Edited by: Amy Ashby

Published by Warren Publishing
Charlotte, NC
www.warrenpublishing.net
Printed in the United States

*"I am me
And I like me
All I want to be is me
Just me."
– Jordyn Downs, age 7*

I am me:

Silly me,

Helpful me,

Adventurous me,

Kind me,

And I like me.

I am me:
Basketball-playing me,

ATV-riding me,

Pencil-sketching me,

And I like me.

I am me:

Tall me,

Jersey-wearing me,

Long, wild-haired me,

Sneaker-sporting me,

Hat-donning me,
And I like me.

I am me.
Some say, "You should be …"

Some say, "Be like me …"
But that's not me.

All I want to be is me.
I like me.

I am me:
Daughter me,

Big sister me,

Older cousin me,

Granddaughter me,

Friend-to-all me,

Printed in the USA
CPSIA information can be obtained
at www.ICGtesting.com
JSHW040237280724
67141JS00003B/7